# Bea Longing

Emily learns anything is possible
(Yes, even during a pandemic!!)
part two

EMILY BEA LONG

Illustrated By

MICHELLE MCDONALD

AuthorHouse™
1663 Liberty Drive
Bloomington, IN 47403
www.authorhouse.com
Phone: 833-262-8899

This book is printed on acid-free paper.

ISBN: 978-1-6655-2181-9 (sc)
978-1-6655-2182-6 (e)

Print information available on the last page.

Published by AuthorHouse 04/13/2021

authorHOUSE®

## *Dedicated to...*

Amanda Long,
Ariana Di Diana,
Maya Brill,
Chan Vong,
Nikki Mescolotto,
Kathleen McDonald,
Tiffany Morrison,
Scott Beyer,
Krystal Miranda,
Caroline Kelly,
Aimee Bushby,
Maddy Wierus,
Kristin Doering,
Michael Cronin,
and Ariana Santizo.

Thank you for brightening my darkest days.

# TABLE OF CONTENTS

# CHAPTER ONE
# ALL YOU NEED IS HEART.

**EMILY** was at Central Park and out popped a rock!
Down she went, tumbling to the ground.
She could feel the stares and glares of others around.
Their snarks and remarks...made her feel sad...
to the bottom of her heart.

She took a seat on the bench.
She was about to give up.
That is—until she heard someone speak.

"Are you Emily Long?"
It was a police officer.
Oh no! She had been caught!
The jig was up.

She'd never become Elmwood Park's Best Singer.
She'd never go to school again.
No one would know where they belong.

"Your mother is worried sick about you. She gave us a call. Lucky for me, a kid riding around E-P on a tricycle isn't too hard to find." said the officer.

"I'm running away from home," said Emily.

That's when Officer Rodriguez realized there was more going on.

"Let me take you home to your mom and I'll let you ride in the police car with me. How does that sound?"

Emily jumped off the bench faster than you can say b-a-n-a-n-a-s.

"Sirens and all?!?!" she said with enthusiasm.

"You got it, kiddo!" replied the officer.

Emily fastened her seatbelt. They were off.

"Why are you running away from home?"

"It's complicated," said Emily.

"Complicated? That sounds like my everyday job. Try me. What's going on?" said Officer Rodriguez.

Emily wasn't sure about opening up.

"Sometimes kids make fun of me because I'm bigger than them," she paused for a moment, then continued. There was more she needed to get off her chest.

"I feel like it's all people see. I want to do something meaningful, but this year has been tough. I feel like I can't do anything right. I want to be Elmwood Park's Best Singer, but I realize I need school too."

"Don't get down on yourself," said Officer Rodriguez.

Emily begins to explain emotions she's been feeling since before the pandemic hit.

"All anyone cares about is how someone looks on the outside, but not about who they are on the inside. What about who I am as a person? What about the person behind this mask?"

"You know, they say the eyes are the window to the soul," said Officer Rodriguez.

"Mr. Officer, my eyes are brown, so I don't know what you're trying to say," said Emily.

She was perplexed.

"Kiddo, when you become someone's friend all anyone cares about is if you can make them laugh."

"I'm not funny," said Emily.

"Are you sure about that?" Officer Rodriguez chuckled. "What matters is who you are on the inside and not what you look like on the outside!"

"Really?" said Emily.

"Sure! There's way more to a person than who they appear to be.

Does it matter if I have red, black, brown, or even blonde hair?"

"You blonde?!"

Emily laughed, "No way!"

She giggled some more, but thought again.

"I guess not!"

Emily was chipper now. He made her feel like she wasn't alone.

"That's because I'm still me. We're all different, but you can't judge a book by its cover. The same goes for you—no matter what you look like! What matters is getting to know someone and learning what makes their heart happy.

People can surprise you when you give them the chance...and if you've got heart and you're as talented as you say you are, there's no stopping you! People will be drawn to you," said Officer Rodriguez.

Emily knew what he was talking about because she felt it.

"I better get back to e-learning, so I can make my dreams come true! Now nothing is holding me back," said Emily.

Officer Rodriguez stopped in front of Emily's home. She jumped out of the car, ran to her steps, and turned around to say, "Bye Mister-Officer!"

He said one last thing before he left, " Some people make good choices. Some people make bad choices. I'm just here to help."

Officer Rodriguez was off and Emily entered her home.
She knew there were some changes she needed to make.

Emily was ready to take the world by storm!
Both e-learning and her dream were still possible.
She knew what she had to do.
Soon everyone would know what it feels like to belong.

# CHAPTER TWO
# COOKIES ARE YUMMY.

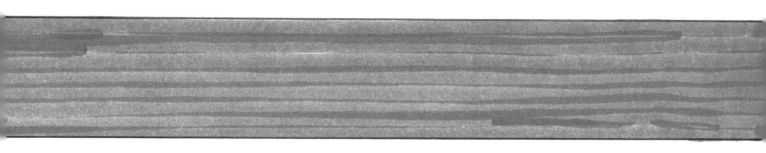

**EMILY** barged through the door with stamina. Determination filled the air.

"Mom, I'm sorry!" she said. "E-learning was tough, but I still want to learn. And if this is how life is at the moment, I know I can do it."

Emily's mom rushed in, gave her a bear hug, and brought her over to the couch.

"Wow, Emily. I'm so proud of you. There's something I'd like to tell you," said her mom.

"What's that?"

"Many people lost their jobs when this virus hit. Many people lost family members and a lot are struggling to cope. They hear about it in the news and on their phones, but this isn't forever.

You're going to grow up and be a big kid. Earth has been around for millions of years. Societies come and go, but the people who live in them, keep living and they keep moving forward."

"You're right mom. I just need to take it one baby step at a time," said Emily.

"Yes, exactly." Then Emily's mom wondered, "Who told you that?"
"Some old lady at the bus stop," she said nonchalantly.
"Wait, what?!"
Emily left the room before her mom could squeeze in another thought!

The next day Emily and her mom were in the kitchen.

"Mom, I love making cookies with you," said Emily.

"Me too. It's important to enjoy life in the moment. Look for those special moments even if there are limits in place."

Emily wanted to let her Mom know how sorry she was for trying to run away.

"Mom, I'm sorry I've been disrespectful."

"I forgive you Emily. These are trying times for everyone. People had to reinvent themselves when the pandemic hit and they're going to have to reinvent themselves again when it's over. We're always changing and evolving."

"It definitely hasn't been easy," said Emily.

"It's okay to feel sad sometimes, but when you're upset let's talk about our feelings openly. I'll always support you."

"Okay Mom. I love you."

"I love you too, sweetie."

# CHAPTER THREE

## DOLPHINS CAN SLEEP WITH ONE EYE OPEN.

**EMILY** started working hard to be
Elmwood Park's best e-learner and best singer.
Turns out—it was easier than she thought!

She started running around the village,
waking up excited for school,
always on time, and she was
brushing her teeth every morning!

Her teachers quickly started
to notice the great changes
Emily was making. She was
student of the month and
they sent a t-shirt to her house!

E-learning wasn't so bad after all.

Emily was kicking major butt in school,
she had no problem wearing
her mask out in public, and she
believed you can still do anything
even with limits in place.

One afternoon after school Emily sprinted into her mom's room and shouted, **"I've learned SO MUCH!**
**I can spell elephant and HIPPOPOTAMUS,**
and did you know
dolphins can sleep with one eye open?!"

"I **TRIED** last night, but I **COULDN'T** do it," said Emily.

"Now it's time to get my **SONG** out there!"

She ran out of the room to play outside. Emily was doing her school work and she was able to make her song too. Even though things had changed, her heart started to feel full again.

Emily found something to belong to.

# CHAPTER FOUR
# FLIPS, FARTS, AND HARD WORK.

**EMILY** met her friend Jimmy and they decided to drink hot cocoa at her house. He was an amazing gymnast. He did flips and cartwheels all the time.

"Jimmy, you make doing flips look so easy. It's AMAZING!" said Emily.

"Thanks, Em. It's not as easy as it looks. I've come a long way."

"I get what you mean. I've worked so hard...what if it's all for nothing? E-learning...my dream to become a singer...I'm working so hard. What if I'm dumb for even trying? I just want to be successful," said Emily.

"Emily, no one is going to give you a hand out in life. That's the way it is, but when you work hard it's rewarding because of the pay off in the end."

Emily knew Jimmy was onto something. He always gave the best advice.

She took a bite of her doughnut and sipped some of her delicious, chocolatey hot cocoa.

"Would I be able to do these flips if everytime I fell I didn't get back up? What if I stayed on the ground after my first fall?"

"You wouldn't be able to flip," said Emily.

"There you go! You have the choice to get back up after you fall. My failures aren't failures. I choose to see them as learning lessons for ways that I can better myself," said Jimmy.

Emily's chest was about to explode. Something inside began to fester.

"What if my parents stop loving me because they think I'm a failure?"she bursted out. The weight of the world lifted off her shoulders.

The truth had finally come out. Jimmy smiled at her.

"Your parents are hard on you because they love you. It's called tough love. Don't let your fear of failure or disappointing them stop you from going after your dream. All you can do is try to be a better person than you were yesterday."

Emily always thought Jimmy could be a poet. He has a way with words unlike anyone else she knows.

"So, go...try...fail...and if you're not some Michaelangelo, that's okay too. Whatever you do, just don't stay on the ground. Get back up. You'll get there eventually," said Jimmy.

"Thanks for knocking some sense into me. You're a true pal," she said.

The pair fist bumped.

"Forever and always. Now go be Elmwood Park's Best Singer. I know you can do it."

"Thanks for lifting me up," she said.

"That's what good friends do."

Emily walked away to grab another doughnut.

Maybe she held the key to her success this whole time? Believing in herself was what Emily needed to do all along. Seeing the great person she was through someone else's eyes gave her the courage to take a leap of faith.

# CHAPTER FIVE

## WHY DIDN'T YOU ASK FOR SHOES OR SOMETHING?

**TODAY'S** the day.

Emily and I are sending our holiday letters to the North Pole.

12-11-2020

Dear Santa,

I really, really hope you get my message in time.

Please tell Rudolph and your elves hello for me. Say hi to Mrs. Claus too!

I'm hoping for a Christmas miracle. Everyone thinks I want to be Elmwood Park's Best Singer, which is only half-true. What I really want is for everyone to know they matter. I want people to know they belong.

Can you make that happen? Please keep it a secret. I'll tell my mom to leave cookies and extra carrots for the reindeer this year.

Sincerely,
Emily Bea

12-11-2020

DEAR SANTY,

1. BARBIES
2. LEGGINGS
3. FOR MY BROTHER TO STOP FARTING ON MY LAP
4. A PUPPY
5. UNICORN
6. A PUPPY AND UNICORN
7. COAL FOR MY BROTHER

DEUCES,
ARIANA

P.S. I'M SORRY I DIDN'T CLEAN UNDER MY BED. PLEASE DON'T GIVE ME COAL. I'LL TAKE CARE OF IT TONIGHT.

"I hope my song makes people smile."

"**WHAT?!?** Why didn't you ask for shoes or something?"

# CHAPTER SIX
## WE ALL BELONG.

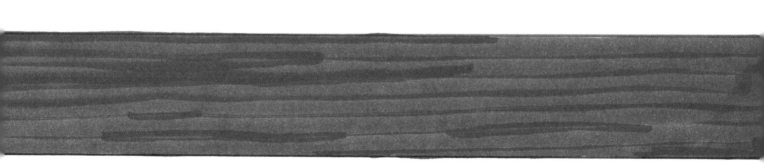

"Emily made her song and it became the talk of the town."

"Alright, Ariana, let me take it from here," said Emily.

"You sure you got this?"

"I think I'm ready."

"I used to think no one believed I could
become the best singer in Elmwood Park.
I thought e-learning and this whole pandemic
was too hard to get through.
The truth is, I never had to be the best.
I learned you only have to try and do your best.

This pandemic has been tough,
but somehow I've managed to get through it.
I'm happy to say it's challenged me in
ways I never thought possible.
I've changed for the better because of it.

You can't let bad moments turn into bad days.
I learned you can do anything you set
your mind to even with limits in place.
That means with or without a mask,
in a classroom or out of a classroom,
at the end of the day, I did it.

I finished this semester with good grades,
I learned a lot, and I was able to make my song.
I don't know if I'll be the best singer in Elmwood Park,
but I can be happy knowing I did my best to
go after something I'm passionate about.

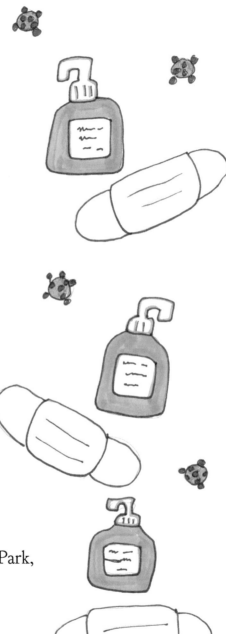

I bet on myself, met some amazing people,
and that's fulfilling a dream for me.
No matter what comes my way
I'm a life-long learner and
I'm going to grab life by the coconuts!"

"Emily, that was beautiful," said Ariana.

"I told you I could," said Emily.

"Are you going to tell them how it ends?"

"Sure, I got this."

"Go for it."

"I needed to change. I needed to grow. Sometimes it takes feeling like the world is against you in order for you to have faith in yourself.

No matter how many bumps come your way, you'll always have some place to call home. I didn't see it before, but during tough times, you can always rely on your community.

I always had a place I belonged, but it took leaving home for me to see it. My home may be Elmwood Park, but it's different for everyone.

We all have a place to belong to, and if you're not sure, step outside and take a look at the people around you. Belonging is more than the roof over your head or where you're standing at the moment. It's your friends, your family, your neighbors...it's your community. Reach out to someone and you'll never be alone because we all belong to each other.

I belong. You belong. We all belong."

# THE END.

# About the Author

**Emily Long** is the author of the new children's book series Bea Longing. Emily is a daycare teacher where she found the inspiration for her first novel. She spends her days caring for students and reminding them their voice matters. Emily has a Bachelor of Science degree in Mass Media from Illinois State University. She knows her name is no coincidence-Emily Bea Long believes everyone belongs.

Visit www.emilybelonging.com to learn more.

Printed in the United States
by Baker & Taylor Publisher Services